When You're Not Looking!

Lynne chapman

GULLANE™ CHILDREN'S BOOKS

Things aren't always
what they seem.
This may look like
a normal scene.

But these creatures
are a crazy crew –
You won't believe
what they all do

...**when
you're not
looking!**

Rhinos love
to wallow,
In squelchy
muddy hollows.

But they
sometimes
use the trees
As a flying
trapeze

...**when
you're not
looking!**

Everyone knows,
Bats
hang from
their toes.

But no-one
ever lets on
They wear
a fez or stetson

...**when
you're not
looking!**

People say that
pigs
are chubby,
Greedy too,
and also grubby.

But they really
are quite chic,
Setting fashions
every week

...when
you're not
looking!

Worms are good at wriggling,
They're not so good at giggling.

But if they put their false teeth in,
They can flash a cheeky grin

...when you're not looking!

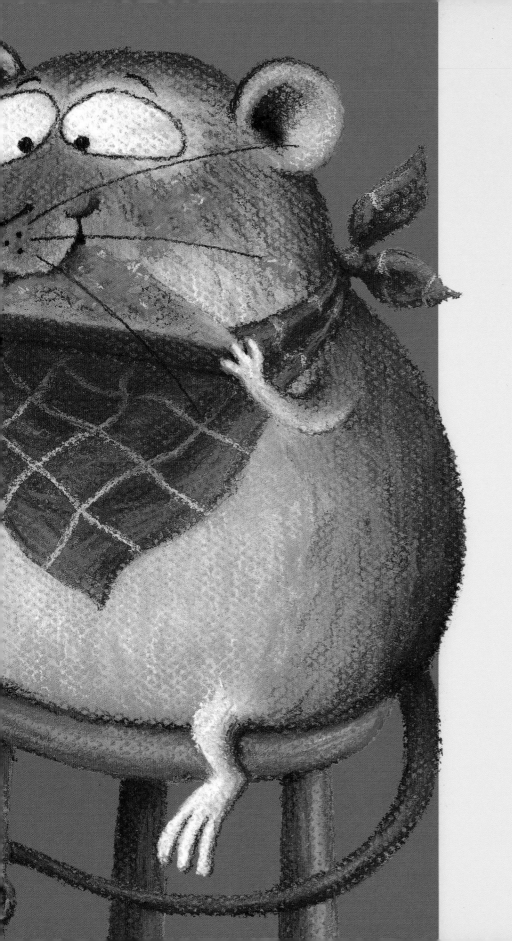

Gerbils play
for hours on end,
By themselves
or with a friend.

But what
they really
love the most
Is eating
marmalade on toast

**...when
you're not
Looking!**

If **COWS** aren't
busy chewing,
They'll most probably
be mooing.

BUT though there
is no proof, they
can rustle up
a soufflé

...when
you're not
Looking!

Snails
as you know,
Always
go slow.

But they
love to change
the pace
With a
turbo-powered race

**...when
you're not
Looking!**

Contented **chickens** peck the ground And make a happy clucking sound.

BUT they love blasting into space, From their hen-house rocket base

...**when you're not Looking!**

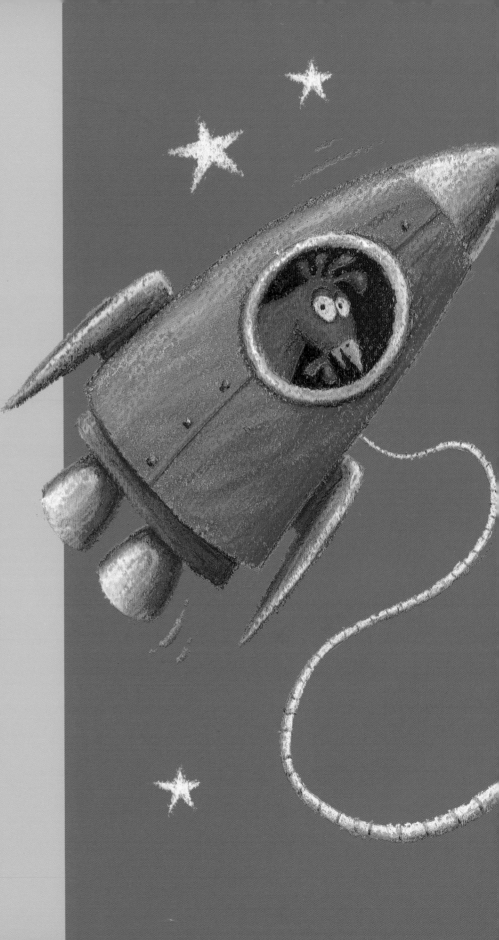